PowerKids Readers:

The Bilingual Library of the United States of America™

Bilingual Edition
English / Spanish
Edición bilingüe

NEVADA

JOSÉ MARÍA OBREGÓN

TRADUCCIÓN AL ESPAÑOL: MARÍA CRISTINA BRUSCA

The Rosen Publishing Group's
PowerKids Press™ & **Editorial Buenas Letras**™
New York

Published in 2006 by The Rosen Publishing Group, Inc.
29 East 21st Street, New York, NY 10010

First Edition

Photo Credits: Cover © Greg Probst/Corbis; p. 5 © Joe Sohm/The Image Works; p. 7 © 2002 Geoatlas; pp. 9, 31 (Arid, Basin) © David Muench/Corbis; p. 11 © Ted Streshinsky/Corbis; p. 13 © Brooklyn Museum of Art/Corbis; p. 15 © Bettmann/Corbis; p. 17 © Lester Lefkowitz/Corbis; p. 19 © Richard Cummins/Corbis; pp. 21, 31 (Land Yacht) © Getty Images; p. 23 © David Butow/Corbis Saba; pp. 25, 30 (Capital) © Reinhard Eisele/Corbis; pp. 26, 30 (Sagebrush) © Craig Tuttle/Corbis; p. 30 (Mountain Bluebird) © David A. Northcott/Corbis; p. 30 (The Silver State) © Killer Stock, Inc./Corbis; p. 30 (Pinyon Pine) © Tom Bean/Corbis; p. 31 (Winnemucca, Stewart) Nevada Historical Society; p. 31 (Garcia) Northeastern Nevada Museum; p. 31 (Newton, Agassi) © Reuters/Corbis; p. 31 (Sepulveda) University of Nevada, Reno

Library of Congress Cataloging-in-Publication Data

Obregón, José María, 1963–
Nevada / José María Obregón ; traducción al español, María Cristina Brusca.— 1st ed.
p. cm. — (The bilingual library of the United States of America) Text in English and Spanish.
Includes bibliographical references (p.) and index.
ISBN 1-4042-3093-9 (library binding)
1. Nevada–Juvenile literature. I. Brusca, María Cristina. II. Title. III. Series.
F841.3.O26 2006
979.3—dc22

2005013789

Manufactured in the United States of America

Due to the changing nature of Internet links, Editorial Buenas Letras has developed an online list of Web sites related to the subject of this book. This site is updated regularly. Please use this link to access the list:

http://www.buenasletraslinks.com/ls/nevada

Contents

Contenido

Welcome to Nevada

These are the flag and seal of the state of Nevada. The name of Nevada comes from the Spanish word meaning "snow-capped." This is because of to the snow-covered mountains of the Sierra Nevada that run through the state.

Bienvenidos a Nevada

Estos son la bandera y el escudo del estado de Nevada. El nombre Nevada significa "cubierta de nieve". Se refiere a la Sierra Nevada cuyas montañas atraviesan el estado y están cubiertas de nieve.

Nevada Flag and State Seal
_____

Bandera y escudo de Nevada

Nevada Geography

In size, Nevada is the seventh-largest state in the nation. Nevada borders the states of California, Oregon, Idaho, Utah and Arizona. Most of Nevada is located in an area called the Great Basin.

Geografía de Nevada

Por su tamaño, Nevada es el séptimo estado de la nación. Nevada linda con los estados de California, Oregón, Idaho, Utah y Arizona. La mayor parte de Nevada ocupa una región llamada la Gran Cuenca.

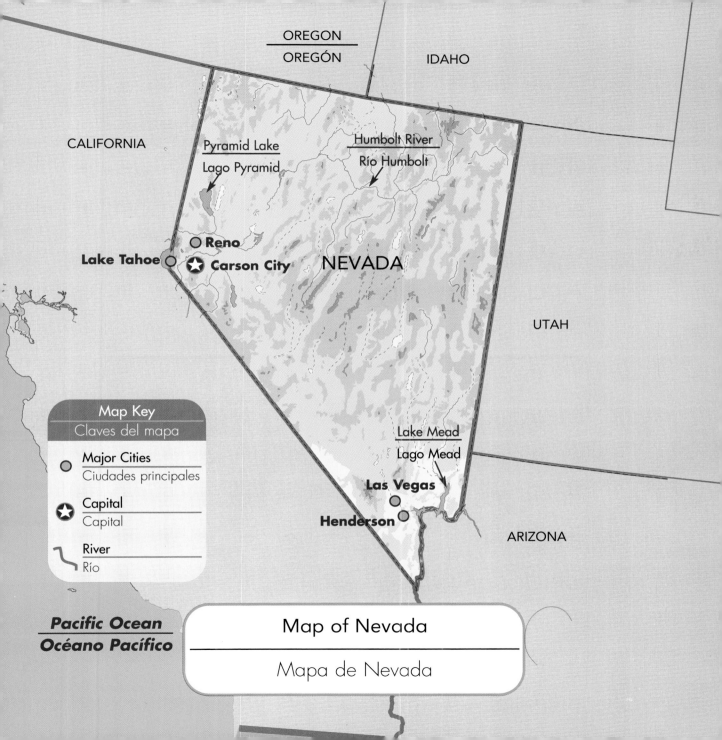

OREGON
OREGÓN

IDAHO

CALIFORNIA

Pyramid Lake
Lago Pyramid

Humbolt River
Río Humbolt

○ Reno

Lake Tahoe ○

☆ Carson City

NEVADA

UTAH

Lake Mead
Lago Mead

Las Vegas
●

Henderson ●

ARIZONA

Map Key
Claves del mapa

○ Major Cities
Ciudades principales

☆ Capital
Capital

River
Río

Pacific Ocean
Océano Pacífico

Map of Nevada

Mapa de Nevada

Nevada is in a mountain region that includes grasslands and sandy deserts. Nevada is the most arid state in the United States. Arid means dry.

Nevada está en una región montañosa que incluye praderas y desiertos de arena. Nevada es el estado más árido de los Estados Unidos. Árido quiere decir seco.

Dry Lake Bed at Black Rock Desert

Fondo seco de un lago en el Desierto Black Rock

Nevada History

Native Americans groups such as the Paiute, the Mojabe, and the Shoshone have lived in Nevada since the early 1800s. Today the state is the home of more than a dozen Native American nations.

Historia de Nevada

Grupos nativoamericanos como los Paiute, Mojabe y Shoshone han vivido en Nevada desde comienzos de 1800. Hoy en día, el estado es el hogar de más de una docena de naciones indígenas.

A Shoshone Family Near Elko, Nevada

Familia Shoshone, cerca de Elko, Nevada

John Charles Frémont was an American army officer and explorer. In the 1830s, Frémont explored the Sierra Nevada. He also studied the Great Basin.

John Charles Frémont fue un oficial del ejército americano y explorador. En la década de 1830, Frémont exploró la Sierra Nevada. También estudió la Gran Cuenca.

General John Charles Frémont

General John Charles Frémont

Nevada is called the Silver State. In 1859, miners found silver in the area known as Comstock. Silver, and later gold, brought a lot of people and money to Nevada.

Nevada es conocido como el Estado de Plata. En 1859, los mineros encontraron plata en una región llamada Comstock. El descubrimiento de plata, y más tarde de oro, atrajo muchas personas y mucho dinero a Nevada.

The Gold Rush in Goldfield, Nevada, 1902

La Fiebre del Oro en Goldfield, Nevada (1902)

In the 1930s Nevada was living through hard times. To create jobs and bring water to the region, the government began construction of the Hoover Dam. The Hoover Dam is one of the world's largest dams.

En la década de 1930, Nevada vivió tiempos difíciles. Para crear trabajos y llevar agua a la región, el gobierno comenzó la construcción de la presa Hoover. La presa Hoover es una de las más grandes del mundo.

Hoover Dam

Presa Hoover

Living in Nevada

Gambling is a popular activity in Nevada. Gambling means to bet money on the result of a game. The state's two main cities, Las Vegas and Reno, attract many visitors.

La vida en Nevada

Los juegos de azar son una actividad muy popular en Nevada. Se apuesta dinero al resultado de un juego. Las dos ciudades principales del estado, Las Vegas y Reno, atraen a muchos visitantes.

Las Vegas Boulevard with Hotels and Casinos

Hoteles y casinos en Las Vegas Boulevard

In Nevada you can go sailing on the Black Rock Desert, without water! You will need a "boat," or land yacht. A Land yacht is a cart with three wheels and a sail. When the winds blows the boat sails away on the dry lake.

¡En Nevada puedes navegar sin agua en el desierto Black Rock! Necesitas un "barco" o velero de tierra. Un velero de tierra es un vehículo que tiene tres ruedas y una vela. Cuando sopla el viento, el velero se desliza sobre el fondo seco del lago.

A Land Yacht on the Black Rock Desert

Velero de tierra en el desierto Black Rock

Nevada Today

People from all over the United States have moved to Nevada. Many Hispanics, or people from Spanish-speaking countries, also live in Nevada. Nevada is growing fast.

Nevada, hoy

Personas de todas partes de los Estados Unidos se han mudado a Nevada. También viven en Nevada muchos hispanos o personas que vienen de países donde se habla el español. Nevada crece muy rápido.

Many New Homes Are Being Built in Nevada

En Nevada se están construyendo muchas viviendas

Las Vegas, Reno, Henderson, and Lake Tahoe are important cities in Nevada. Carson City is the capital of the state.

Las Vegas, Reno, Henderson y Lake Tahoe son ciudades importantes de Nevada. Carson City es la capital del estado.

Capitol Building in Carson City

Capitolio de Carson City

Activity:
Let's Draw Nevada's State Flower

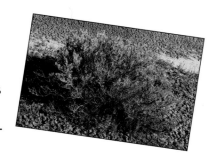

The sagebrush *(Artemisia Tridentata)* **became Nevada's official flower in 1967.**

Actividad:
Dibujemos la flor del estado de Nevada

La artemisa es la flor oficial del estado de Nevada desde 1967.

1

Begin by drawing some wavy lines for the winding branches.

Comienza por trazar algunas líneas curvas para dibujar las ramas onduladas.

2

Next add a lot of leaves. They have a special curved shape, so follow the picture carefully.

Luego, agrega muchas hojas. Las hojas tienen una forma curvada especial. Copia con cuidado la figura de la muestra.

3

Add the vein that goes down the center of each leaf.

Agrega la vena central de cada hoja.

4

Shade the branches so that they appear dark.

Sombrea las ramas de manera que se vean oscuras.

5

Add more veins to each leaf. Great job!

Agrega más venas en cada hoja. ¡Bien hecho!

27

Timeline

Timeline		Cronología
Anasazi tribes build in Nevada.	A.D. 500–1500 d.C	Las tribus Anasazi construyen en Nevada.
José Antonio Armijo crosses Nevada.	1829	José Antonio Armijo cruza Nevada.
Silver is found in Comstock.	1859	Se encuentra plata en Comstock.
Nevada becomes a state.	1864	Nevada se convierte en estado.
Nevada women get the right to vote.	1914	Las mujeres de Nevada adquieren el derecho a votar.
Gambling is legalized.	1931	Se legaliza el juego de azar.
The Hoover Dam is completed.	1936	Se completa la presa Hoover.
Great Basin National Park is created.	1986	Se crea el Parque Nacional de la Gran Cuenca.
U.S. Congress approves the use of Yucca Mountain as the nation's waste dump.	2002	El congreso de E.U.A. aprueba el uso del Monte Yucca como basurero nuclear de la nación.

Nevada Events

April
Native American Arts Festival in Henderson

May
ArtFest in Henderson

June
Naval Air Station Air Show in Fallon
Reno Rodeo

July
Winnemucca Fifties Fever automobile parade

August
Tahoe/Reno International Film Festival

September
The Great Reno Balloon Race

October
Art in the Park in Boulder City

November
Veteran's Day Parade in Mesquite

Eventos en Nevada

Abril
Festival de arte nativoamericano, en Henderson

Mayo
Artfest, en Henderson

Junio
Exposición de aeronáutica de la Estación Aérea Naval, en Fallon
Rodeo de Reno

Julio
Desfile de automóviles Winnemucca Fifties Fever

Agosto
Festival internacional de cine de Tahoe/Reno

Septiembre
Gran carrera de globos de Reno

Octubre
Arte en el parque, en Boulder City

Noviembre
Desfile del día del veterano, en Mesquite

Nevada Facts/Datos sobre Nevada

<u>Population</u>
1.9 million

<u>Población</u>
1.9 millones

<u>Capital</u>
Carson City

<u>Capital</u>
Carson City

<u>State Motto</u>
All for Our Country

<u>Lema del estado</u>
Todo por nuestro país

<u>State Flower</u>
Sagebrush

<u>Flor del estado</u>
Artemisa

<u>State Bird</u>
Mountain bluebird

<u>Ave del estado</u>
Azulejo de la montaña

<u>State Nickname</u>
The Silver State

<u>Mote del estado</u>
El Estado de Plata

<u>State Trees</u>
Single-leaf pinyon
and bristlecone pine

<u>Árboles del estado</u>
Piñonero de hoja
sencilla y pino longevo

<u>State Song</u>
"Home Means
Nevada"

<u>Canción del estado</u>
"Hogar quiere decir
Nevada"

30

Famous Nevadans/Nevadenses famosos

Sarah Winnemucca
(1844–1891)
Author and educator
Escritora y educadora

Helen Stewart
(1854–1926)
Community leader
Líder comunitaria

G. S. Garcia
(1864–1933)
Businessman
Empresario

Wayne Newton
(1942–)
Entertainer
Animador

Emma Sepúlveda
(1950–)
Author, community leader
Escritora y líder comunitaria

Andre Agassi
(1970–)
Tennis player
Jugador de tenis

Words to Know/Palabras que debes saber

arid
árido

basin
cuenca

border
frontera

land yacht
velero de tierra

31

Here are more books to read about Nevada:
Otros libros que puedes leer sobre Nevada:

In English/En inglés:

Nevada
From Sea to Shining Sea
by Williams, Suzanne
Children's Press, 2003

Nevada
Hello U.S.A.
by Sirvaitis, Karen
Lerner Publishing Group, 2002

Words in English: 355   Palabras en español: 378

Index

Índice